SUNNY
AND
THE BIRDS

WENDY MEDDOUR

NABILA ADANI

OXFORD
UNIVERSITY PRESS

Every evening, Sunny and Daddy looked out at the birds. 'Do you know what those fast ones are called?' asked Daddy.

'Of course I do,' said Sunny. 'They're swallows.'

'We used to have swallows back home,' sighed Daddy. 'They would swoop in the tangerine skies.'

'But this is our home!' said Sunny,
pointing at the rug under his feet.

'I know.' Daddy ruffled Sunny's hair.

The next day, when Sunny
woke up, there was a pretty
grey bird cooing in the garden.

'Do you know what it is?'
asked Daddy.

'A type of dove,' grinned Sunny.

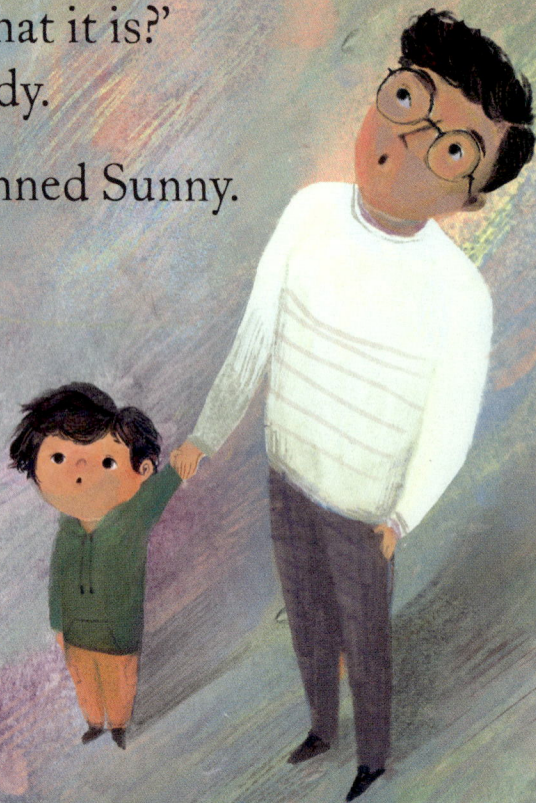

'Yes. It's a collared dove,' said Daddy.
'Just like the ones back home.
They used to "coooo" in the soft morning light!'

'But this is our home,' sighed Sunny.

That night, Sunny couldn't sleep,
so he crept downstairs.

Daddy was still sitting at
the kitchen table.

'We're like two old owls,' said Daddy, making Sunny some warm milk. 'Just like the brown wood owls that used to nest in the trees behind our home.'

'But this is our home,' said Sunny, banging the surface with his hand.

The next night, Sunny couldn't sleep again.

Nor could Daddy.

'Apart from owls,' asked Daddy, 'what other birds stay up in the night?'

Sunny thought very hard.

'Ones that are feeling sad?' he asked.

Daddy didn't say anything but held
Sunny close and breathed in his hair.

The next day, it was Nanna Anissa's turn
to collect Sunny from school.

'Can we buy Daddy a present,
please?' asked Sunny.

'Of course,' smiled Nanna Anissa.
'What would you like to buy?'

'A surprise.' Sunny whispered
into his nanna's ear.

'Close your eyes, Daddy,' said Sunny, leading him into the garden later that afternoon.

'What is it?' asked Daddy,
stumbling over the clumps of grass.

'Wait and see,' grinned Sunny.

There, underneath the apple tree,
was a bird table and a feeder
full of seeds.

Daddy blinked. 'Oh!
It's wonderful,' he said.

That night, Daddy and Sunny
both felt very, very sleepy.

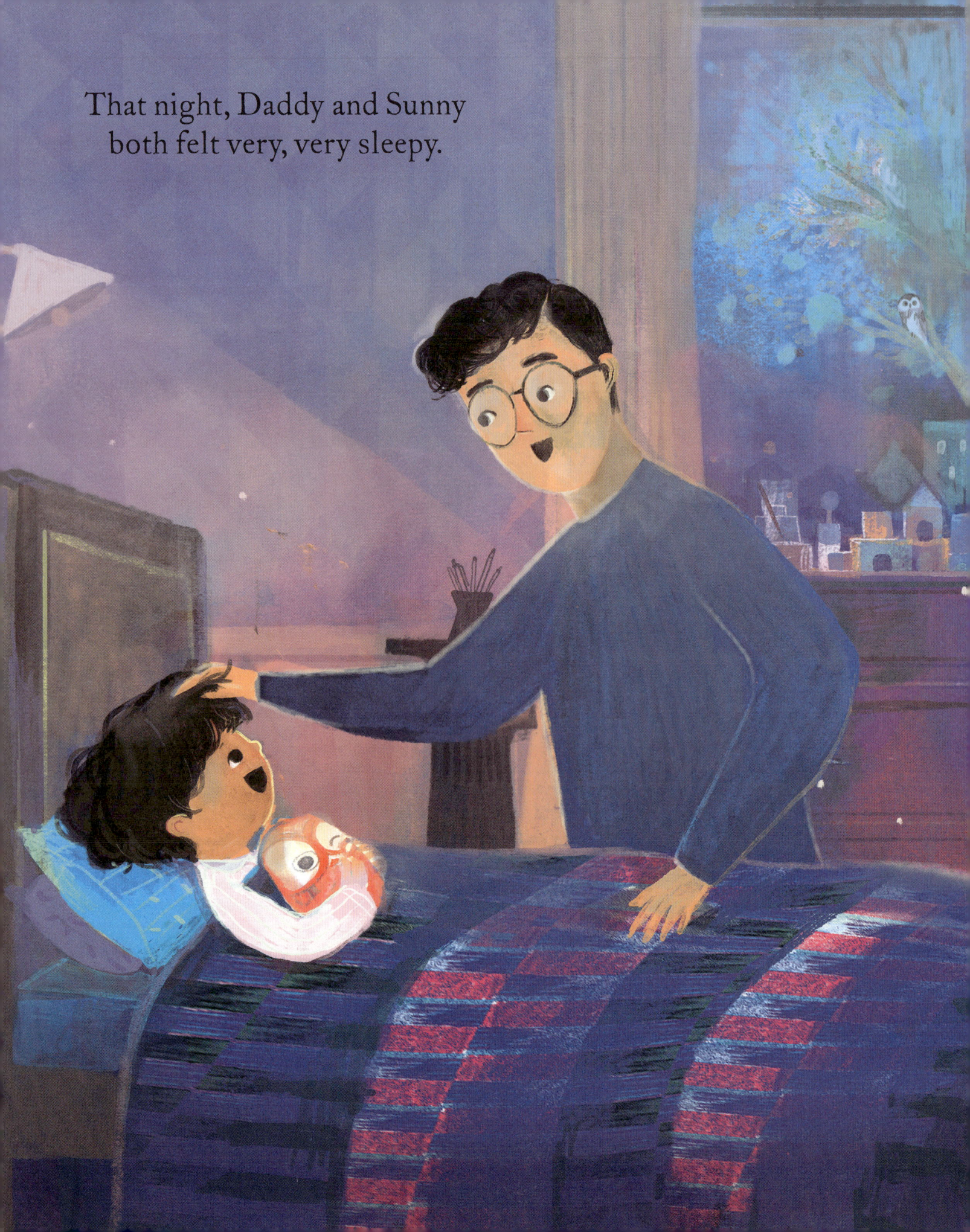

'Can you think of any birds that sleep
through the night?' asked Daddy,
tucking Sunny up in bed.

'Happy ones,' beamed Sunny.

The next morning, Daddy and
Sunny ran downstairs and looked
through the kitchen window.

'What can you see?'
asked Sunny.

'I can see 3 goldfinches,
2 blue tits,
1 greenfinch,
and . . . wait . . . wait . . .

I don't believe it . . .
and a great spotted
woodpecker!'

said Daddy, writing
them all down.

'Can we always remember
to feed them?' asked Sunny.

'Yes,' said Daddy.
'Then, even if they fly
away, they'll always
come back home.'

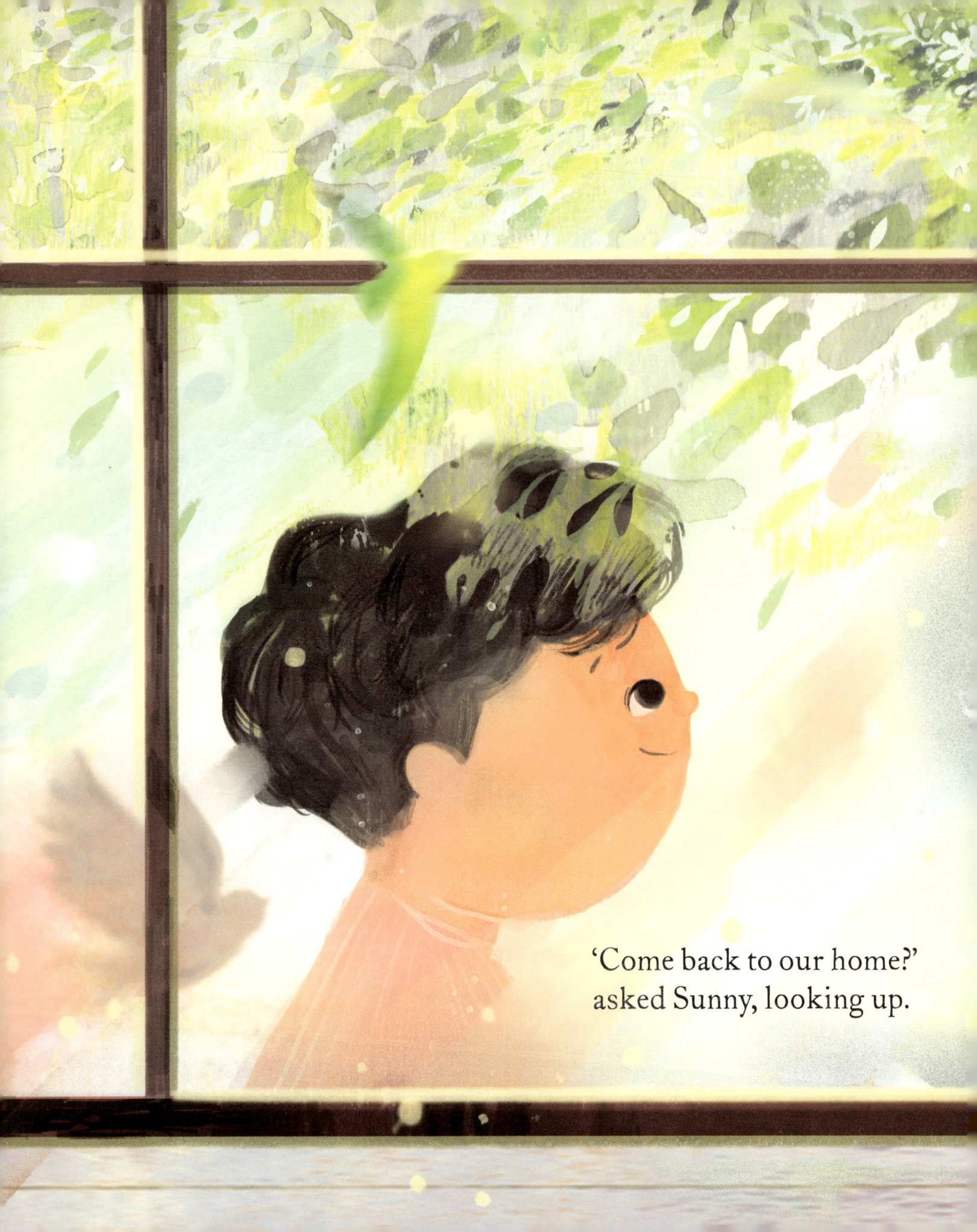

'Come back to our home?' asked Sunny, looking up.

'Yes, Sunny,'
beamed Daddy . . .

'Back to
OUR
home.'

swallow

blackbird

blue tit

greenfinch

goldfinch